Figures
of Earth

Figures of Earth

A Comedy of Appearances

By
JAMES BRANCH CABELL

"Cascun se mir el jove Manuel,
Qu'era del mon lo plus valens dels pros."

NEW YORK
ROBERT M. McBRIDE & CO.
1926

Seventh Printing, November, 1926

*Printed in the
United States of America*

Published, February, 1921

TO SIX MOST GALLANT CHAMPIONS IS DEDICATED
THIS HISTORY OF A CHAMPION: LESS TO REPAY
THAN TO ACKNOWLEDGE LARGE DEBTS TO EACH
OF THEM, COLLECTIVELY AT OUTSET, AS THERE-
AFTER SERIATIM.

Contents

A FOREWORD

"Amoto quæramus seria ludo."

TO
SINCLAIR LEWIS.

A Foreword

My dear Lewis:

To you (whom I take to be as familiar with the Manuelian cycle of romance as is any person now alive) it has for some while appeared, I know, a not uncurious circumstance that in the *Key to the Popular Tales of Poictesme* there should have been included so little directly relative to Manuel himself. No reader of the *Popular Tales* (as I recall your saying at the Alum when we talked over, among so many other matters, this monumental book) can fail to note that always Dom Manuel looms obscurely in the background, somewhat as do King Arthur and white-bearded Charlemagne in their several cycles, dispensing justice and bestowing rewards, and generally arranging the future, for the survivors of the outcome of stories which more intimately concern themselves with Anavalt and Coth and Holden, or even with Sclaug and Thragnar, than with the liege-lord of Poictesme. Except in the old sixteenth-century chap-book (unknown to you, I believe, and never reprinted since 1822, and not ever modernized into any cognizable spelling), there seems to have been nowhere an

English rendering of the legends in which Dom
Manuel is really the main figure.

Well, this book attempts to supply that desider-
atum, and is, so far as the writer is aware, the one
fairly complete epitome in modern English of the
Manuelian historiography not included by Lewistam
which has yet been prepared.

It is obvious, of course, that in a single volume
of this bulk there could not be included more than
a selection from the great body of myths which, we
may assume, have accumulated gradually round the
mighty though shadowy figure of Manuel the Re-
deemer. Instead, my aim has been to make choice
of such stories and traditions as seemed most fit to
be cast into the shape of a connected narrative and
regular sequence of events; to lend to all that wholesome, edifying and optimistic tone which in read-
ing-matter is so generally preferable to mere intelligence; and meanwhile to preserve as much of
the quaint style of the gestes as is consistent with
clearness. Then, too, in the original mediæval
romances, both in their prose and metrical form,
there are occasional allusions to natural processes
which make these stories unfit to be placed in the
hands of American readers, who, as a body, attest
their respectability by insisting that their parents
were guilty of unmentionable conduct; and such
passages of course necessitate considerable editing.

2

No schoolboy (and far less the scholastic
chronicler of those last final upshots for whose
furtherance "Hannibal invaded Rome and Erasmus
wrote in Oxford cloisters") needs nowadays to be
told that the Manuel of these legends is to all intents
a fictitious person. That in the earlier half of the
thirteenth century there was ruling over the Poic-
toumois a powerful chieftain named Manuel, nobody has of late disputed seriously. But the events
of the actual human existence of this Lord of
Poictesme—very much as the Emperor Frederick
Barbarossa has been identified with the wood-demon
Barbatos, and the prophet Elijah, "caught up into
the chariot of the Vedic Vayu," has become one
with the Slavonic Perun,—have been inextricably
blended with the legends of the Dirghic Manu-Elul,
Lord of August.

Thus even the irregularity in Manuel's eyes is
taken by Vanderhoffen, in his *Tudor Tales,* to be a
myth connecting Manuel with the Vedic Rudra
and the Russian Magarko and the Servian Vii,—
"and every beneficent storm-god represented with
his eye perpetually winking (like sheet lightning),
lest his concentrated look (the thunderbolt) should
reduce the universe to ashes. . . . His watery
parentage, and the storm-god's relationship with a

swan-maiden of the Apsarasas (typifying the mists and clouds), and with Freydis the fire queen, are equally obvious: whereas Niafer is plainly a variant of Nephthys, Lady of the House, whose personality Dr. Budge sums up as 'the goddess of the death which is not eternal,' or Nerthus, the Subterranean Earth, which the warm rain-storm quickens to life and fertility."

All this seems dull enough to be plausible. Yet no less an authority than Charles Garnier has replied, in rather indignant rebuttal: "Qu'ont été en réalité Manuel et Siegfried, Achille et Rustem? Par quels exploits ont-ils mérité l'éternelle admiration que leur ont vouée les hommes de leur race? Nul ne répondra jamais à ces questions. . . . Mais Poictesme croit à la réalité de cette figure que ses romans ont faite si belle, car le pays n'a pas d'autre histoire. Cette figure du Comte Manuel est réelle d'ailleurs, car elle est l'image purifiée de la race qui l'a produite, et, si on peut s'exprimer ainsi, l'incarnation de son génie."

—Which is quite just, and, when you come to think it over, proves Dom Manuel to be nowadays, for practical purposes, at least as real as Dr. Paul Vanderhoffen.

3

Between the two main epic cycles of Poictesme,

as embodied in *Les Gestes de Manuel* and *La Haulte Histoire de Jurgen,* more or less comparison is inevitable: and therefore it is to be hoped that the Jurgen epos may some day be made accessible to American readers.

Says Codman: "The Gestes are mundane stories, the History is a cosmic affair, in that, where Manuel faces the world, Jurgen considers the universe. . . . Dom Manuel is the Achilles of Poictesme, as Jurgen is its Ulysses."

Now, roughly, the distinction serves. Yet minute consideration discovers, I think, in these two sets of legends a more profound, if subtler, difference, in the handling of the protagonist: with Jurgen all of the physical and mental man is rendered as a matter of course; whereas in dealing with Manuel there is, always, I believe, a certain perceptible and strange, if not inexplicable, aloofness. Manuel did thus and thus, Manuel said so and so, these legends recount: yes, but never anywhere have I detected any firm assertion as to Manuel's thoughts and emotions, nor any peep into the workings of this hero's mind. He is "done" from the outside, always at arm's length. It is not merely that Manuel's nature is tinctured with the cool unhumanness of his father the water-demon: rather, these old poets of Poictesme would seem, whether of intention or no, to have dealt with their

national hero as an admirable person whom they
have never been able altogether to love, or entirely
to sympathize with, or to view quite without dis-
trust.

There are several ways of accounting for this
fact,—ranging from the hurtful as well as beneficent aspect of the storm-god, to the natural in-
ability of a poet to understand a man who succeeds
in everything: but the fact is, after all, of no present importance save that it may well have prompted
Lewistam to scamp his dealings with this always
somewhat ambiguous Manuel, and so to omit the
hereinafter included legends, as unsuited to the
clearer and sunnier atmosphere of the *Popular
Tales*.

For my part, I am quite content, in this Comedy
of Appearances, to follow the old romancers' lead.
"Such and such things were said and done by our
great Manuel," they say to us, in effect: "such and
such were the appearances, and do you make what
you can of them."

I say that, too, with the addition that in real life,
also, such is the fashion in which we are compelled
to deal with all happenings and with all our fellows,
whether they wear or lack the gaudy name of
heroism.

Dumbarton Grange
October, 1920.

PART ONE

THE BOOK OF CREDIT

TO
WILSON FOLLETT.

"Then answered the Sorcerer dredefully: Manuel, Manuel, now I shall shewe unto thee many bokes of *Nygromancy,* and howe thou shalt cum by it lyghtly and knowe the practyse therein. And, moreouer, I shall shewe and informe you so that thou shalt haue thy Desyre, whereby my thynke it is a great Gyfte for so lytyll a doynge."

I.

How Manuel Left the Mire

THEY of Poictesme narrate that in the old days when miracles were as common as fruit pies, young Manuel was a swineherd, living modestly in attendance upon the miller's pigs. They tell also that Manuel was content enough: he knew not of the fate which was reserved for him.

Meanwhile in all the environs of Rathgor, and in the thatched villages of Lower Targamon, he was well liked: and when the young people gathered in the evening to drink brandy and eat nuts and gingerbread, nobody danced more merrily than Squinting Manuel. He had a quiet way with the girls, and with the men a way of solemn, blinking simplicity which caused the more hasty in judgment to consider him a fool. Then, too, young Manuel was very often detected smiling sleepily over nothing, and his gravest care in life appeared to be that figure which Manuel had made out of marsh clay from the pool of Haranton.

This figure he was continually reshaping and re-altering. The figure stood upon the margin of the pool; and near by were two stones overgrown with

3

moss, and supporting a cross of old worm-eaten wood, which commemorated what had been done there.

One day, toward autumn, as Manuel was sitting in this place, and looking into the deep still water, a stranger came, and he wore a fierce long sword that interfered deplorably with his walking.

"Now I wonder what it is you find in that dark pool to keep you staring so?" the stranger asked, first of all.

"I do not very certainly know," replied Manuel, "but mistily I seem to see drowned there the loves and the desires and the adventures I had when I wore another body than this. For the water of Haranton, I must tell you, is not like the water of other fountains, and curious dreams engender in this pool."

"I speak no ill against oneirology, although broad noon is hardly the best time for its practise," declared the snub-nosed stranger. "But what is that thing?" he asked, pointing.

"It is the figure of a man, which I have modeled and re-modeled, sir, but cannot seem to get exactly to my liking. So it is necessary that I keep laboring at it until the figure is to my thinking and my desire."

"But, Manuel, what need is there for you to model it at all?"

"Because my mother, sir, was always very anxious for me to make a figure in the world, and when she lay a-dying I promised her that I would do so, and then she put a geas upon me to do it."

"Ah, to be sure! but are you certain it was this kind of figure she meant?"

"Yes, for I have often heard her say that, when I grew up, she wanted me to make myself a splendid and admirable young man in every respect. So it is necessary that I make the figure of a young man, for my mother was not of these parts, but a woman of Ath Cliath, and so she put a geas upon me—"

"Yes, yes, you had mentioned this geas, and I am wondering what sort of a something is this geas."

"It is what you might call a bond or an obligation, sir, only it is of the particularly strong and unreasonable and secret sort which the Firbolg use."

The stranger now looked from the figure to Manuel, and the stranger deliberated the question (which later was to puzzle so many people) if any human being could be as simple as Manuel appeared. Manuel at twenty was not yet the burly giant he became. But already he was a gigantic and florid person, so tall that the heads of few men reached to his shoulder; a person of handsome exterior, high featured and blond, having a narrow small head, and vivid light blue eyes, and the chest of a stallion; a person whose left eyebrow had an odd oblique droop, so that the stupendous boy at his simplest appeared to be winking the information that he was in jest.

All in all, the stranger found this young swineherd ambiguous; and there was another curious thing too which the stranger noticed about Manuel.

"Is it on account of this geas," asked the stranger, "that a great lock has been sheared away from your yellow hair?"

In an instant Manuel's face became dark and wary. "No," he said, "that has nothing to do with my geas, and we must not talk about that."

"Now you are a queer lad to be having such an obligation upon your head, and to be having wellnigh half the hair cut away from your head, and to be having inside your head such notions. And while small harm has ever come from humoring one's mother, yet I wonder at you, Manuel, that you should sit here sleeping in the sunlight among your pigs, and be giving your young time to improbable sculpture and stagnant water, when there is such a fine adventure awaiting you, and when the Norns are foretelling such high things about you as they spin the thread of your living."

"Hah, glory be to God, friend, but what is this adventure?"

"The adventure is that the Count of Arnaye's daughter yonder has been carried off by a wizard, and that the high Count Demetrios offers much wealth and broad lands, and his daughter's hand in marriage too, to the lad that will fetch back this lovely girl."

"I have heard talk of this in the kitchen of Arnaye, where I sometimes sell them a pig. But what are such matters to a swineherd?"

"My lad, you are to-day a swineherd drowsing in the sun, as yesterday you were a baby squalling in the cradle, but to-morrow you will be neither of these if there be any truth whatever in the talking of the Norns as they gossip at the foot of their ash-tree."

Manuel appeared to accept the inevitable. He bowed his brightly colored high head, saying gravely: "All honor be to Urdhr and Verdandi and Skuld! If I am decreed to be the champion that is to rescue the Count of Arnaye's daughter, it is ill arguing with the Norns. Come, tell me now, how do you call this doomed wizard, and how does one get to him to sever his wicked head from his foul body?"

"Men speak of him as Miramon Lluagor, lord of the nine kinds of sleep and prince of the seven madnesses. He lives in mythic splendor at the top of the gray mountain called Vraidex, where he contrives all manner of illusions, and, in particular, designs the dreams of men."

"Yes, in the kitchen of Arnaye, also, such was the report concerning this Miramon: and not a person in the kitchen denied that this Miramon is an ugly customer."

"He is the most subtle of wizards. None can withstand him, and nobody can pass the terrible serpentine designs which Miramon has set to guard the gray scarps of Vraidex unless one carries the more terrible sword Flamberge, which I have here in its blue scabbard."

"Why, then, it is you who must rescue the Count's daughter."

"No, that would not do at all: for there is in the life of a champion too much of turmoil and of buffetings and murderings to suit me, who am a peace-loving person. Besides, to the champion who rescues the Lady Gisèle will be given her hand in marriage, and as I have a wife, I know that to have two wives would lead to twice too much dissension to suit me, who am a peace-loving person. So I think it is you who had better take the sword and the adventure."

"Well," Manuel said, "much wealth and broad lands and a lovely wife are finer things to ward than a parcel of pigs."

So Manuel girded on the charmed scabbard, and with the charmed sword he sadly demolished the clay figure he could not get quite right. Then

Manuel sheathed Flamberge, and Manuel cried farewell to the pigs.

"I shall not ever return to you, my pigs, because, at worst, to die valorously is better than to sleep out one's youth in the sun. A man has but one life. It is his all. Therefore I now depart from you, my pigs, to win me a fine wife and much wealth and leisure wherein to discharge my geas. And when my geas is lifted I shall not come back to you, my pigs, but I shall travel everywhither, and into the last limits of earth, so that I may see the ends of this world and may judge them while my life endures. For after that, they say, I judge not, but am judged: and a man whose life has gone out of him, my pigs, is not even good bacon."

"So much rhetoric for the pigs," says the stranger, "is well enough, and likely to please them. But come, is there not some girl or another to whom you should be saying good-bye with other things than words?"

"No, at first I thought I would also bid farewell to Suskind, who is sometimes friendly with me in the twilight wood, but upon reflection it seems better not to. For Suskind would probably weep, and exact promises of eternal fidelity, and otherwise dampen the ardor with which I look toward tomorrow and the winning of the wealthy Count of Arnaye's lovely daughter."

"Now, to be sure, you are a queer cool candid fellow, you young Manuel, who will go far, whether for good or evil!"

"I do not know about good or evil. But I am Manuel, and I shall follow after my own thinking and my own desires."

"And certainly it is no less queer you should be saying that: for, as everybody knows, it used to be the favorite byword of your namesake the famous Count Manuel that is so newly dead in the South yonder."

At that the young swineherd nodded gravely. "I must accept the omen, sir. For, as I interpret it, my great namesake has courteously made way for me, in order that I may go far beyond him."

Then Manuel cried farewell and thanks to the mild-mannered, snub-nosed stranger, and Manuel left the miller's pigs to their own devices by the pool of Haranton, and Manuel marched away in his rags to meet a fate that was long talked about.

2.

Niafer

THE first thing of all that Manuel did, was to fill a knapsack with simple and nutritious food, and then he went to the gray mountain called Vraidex, upon the remote and cloud-wrapped summit of which dread Miramon Lluagor dwelt, in a doubtful palace wherein the lord of the nine sleeps contrived illusions and designed the dreams of men. When Manuel had passed under some very old maple-trees, and was beginning the ascent, he found a smallish, flat-faced, dark-haired boy going up before him.

"Hail, snip," says Manuel, "and whatever are you doing in this perilous place?"

"Why, I am going," the dark-haired boy replied, "to find out how the Lady Gisèle d'Arnaye is faring on the tall top of this mountain."

"Oho, then we will undertake this adventure together, for that is my errand too. And when the adventure is fulfilled, we will fight together, and the survivor will have the wealth and broad lands and the Count's daughter to sit on his knee. What do they call you, friend?"

"I am called Niafer. But I believe that the Lady Gisèle is already married, to Miramon Lluagor. At least, I sincerely hope she is married to this wizard, for otherwise it would not be respectable for her to be living with him at the top of this gray mountain."

"Fluff and puff! what does that matter?" says Manuel. "There is no law against a widow's re-marrying forthwith: and widows are quickly made by any champion about whom the wise Norns are already talking. But I must not tell you about that, Niafer, because I do not wish to appear boastful. So I must simply say to you, Niafer, that I am called Manuel, and have no other title as yet, being not yet even a baron."

"Come now," says Niafer, "but you are rather sure of yourself for a young boy!"

"Why, of what may I be sure in this shifting world if not of myself?"

"Our elders, Manuel, declare that such self-conceit is a fault, and our elders, they say, are wiser than we."

"Our elders, Niafer, have long had the management of this world's affairs, and you can see for yourself what they have made of these affairs. What sort of a world is it, I ask you, in which time peculates the gold from hair and the crimson from all lips, and the north wind carries away the glow and glory and contentment of October, and a drivel-

ing old wizard steals a lovely girl? Why, such
maraudings are out of reason, and show plainly that
our elders have no notion how to manage things."

"Eh, Manuel, and will you re-model the world?"

"Who knows?" says Manuel, in the high pride
of his youth. "At all events, I do not mean to
leave it unaltered."

Then Niafer, a more prosaic person, gave him a
long look compounded equally of admiration and
pity, but Niafer did not dispute the matter. Instead, these two pledged constant fealty until they
should have rescued Madame Gisèle.

"Then we will fight for her," says Manuel, again.

"First, Manuel, let me see her face, and then let
me see her state of mind, and afterward I will see
about fighting you. Meanwhile, this is a very tall
mountain, and the climbing of it will require all the
breath which we are wasting here."

So the two began the ascent of Vraidex, by the
winding road upon which the dreams travel when
they are sent down to men by the lord of the seven
madnesses. All gray rock was the way at first.
But they soon reached the gnawed bones of those
who had ascended before them, scattered about a
small plain that was overgrown with ironweed: and
through and over the tall purple blossoms came to
destroy the boys the Serpent of the East, a very
dreadful design with which Miramon afflicts the

sleep of Lithuanians and Tatars. The snake rode on a black horse, a black falcon perched on his head, and a black hound followed him. The horse stumbled, the falcon clamored, the hound howled.

Then said the snake: "My steed, why do you stumble? my hound, why do you howl? and my falcon, why do you clamor? For these three doings foresay some ill to me."

"Oh, a great ill!" replies Manuel, with his charmed sword out.

But Niafer cried: "An endless ill is foresaid by these doings. For I have been to the Island of the Oaks: and under the twelfth oak was a copper casket, and in the casket was a purple duck, and in the duck was an egg: and in the egg, O Norka, was and is your death."

"It is true that my death is in such an egg," said the Serpent of the East, "but nobody will ever find that egg, and therefore I am resistless and immortal."

"To the contrary, the egg, as you can perceive, is in my hand; and when I break this egg you will die, and it is smaller worms than you that will be thanking me for their supper this night."

The serpent looked at the poised egg, and he trembled and writhed so that his black scales scattered everywhither scintillations of reflected sunlight. He cried, "Give me the egg, and I will permit you two to pass unmolested to a more terrible destruction."

Niafer was not eager to do this, but Manuel thought it best, and so at last Niafer consented to the bargain, for the sake of the serpent's children. Then the two lads went upward, while the serpent bandaged the eyes of his horse and of his hound, and hooded his falcon, and crept gingerly away to hide the egg in an unmentionable place.

"But how in the devil," says Manuel, "did you manage to come by that invaluable egg?"

"It is a quite ordinary duck egg, Manuel. But the Serpent of the East has no way of discovering that unless he breaks the egg: and that is the one thing the serpent will never do, because he thinks it is the magic egg which contains his death."

"Come, Niafer, you are not handsome to look at, but you are far cleverer than I thought you!"

Now as Manuel clapped Niafer on the shoulder, the forest beside the roadway was agitated, and the underbrush crackled, and the tall beech-trees crashed and snapped and tumbled helter-skelter. The crust of the earth was thus broken through by the Serpent of the North. Only the head and throat of this design of Miramon's was lifted from the jumbled trees, for it was requisite of course that the serpent's lower coils should never loose their grip upon the foundations of Norroway. All of the design that showed was overgrown with seaweed and barnacles.

"It is the will of Miramon Lluagor that I forthwith demolish you both," says this serpent, yawning with a mouth like a fanged cave.

Once more young Manuel had brandished his charmed sword Flamberge, but it was Niafer who spoke.

"No, for before you can destroy me," says Niafer, "I shall have cast this bridle over your head."

"What sort of bridle is that?" inquired the great snake scornfully.

"And are those goggling flaming eyes not big enough and bright enough to see that this is the soft bridle called Gleipnir, which is made of the breath of fish and of the spittle of birds and of the footfall of a cat?"

"Now, although certainly such a bridle was foretold," the snake conceded, a little uneasily, "how can I make sure that you speak the truth when you say this particular bridle is Gleipnir?"

"Why, in this way: I will cast the bridle over your head, and then you will see for yourself that the old prophecy will be fulfilled, and that all power and all life will go out of you, and that the Northmen will dream no more."

"No, do you keep that thing away from me, you

little fool! No, no: we will not test your truthfulness in that way. Instead, do you two go your way to a more terrible destruction, and to face barbaric dooms coming from the west. And do you give me the bridle to demolish in place of you. And then, if I live forever I shall know that this is indeed Gleipnir, and that you have spoken the truth."

So Niafer consented to this testing of his veracity, rather than permit this snake to die, and the foundations of Norroway (in which kingdom, Niafer confessed, he had an aunt then living) thus to be dissolved by the loosening of the dying serpent's grip upon Middlegarth. The bridle was yielded, and Niafer and Manuel went upward.

Manuel asked, "Snip, was that in truth the bridle called Gleipnir?"

"No, Manuel, it is an ordinary bridle. But the Serpent of the North has no way of discovering this except by fitting the bridle over his head: and this one thing the serpent will never do, because he knows that then, if my bridle proved to be Gleipnir, all power and all life would go out of him."

"O subtle, ugly little snip!" says Manuel: and again he patted Niafer on the shoulder. Then Manuel spoke very highly in praise of cleverness, and said that, for one, he had never objected to it in its place.

3.

Ascent of Vraidex

NOW it was evening, and the two sought shelter in a queer windmill by the roadside, finding there a small wrinkled old man in a patched coat. He gave them lodgings for the night, and honest bread and cheese, but for his own supper he took frogs out of his bosom, and roasted these in the coals.

Then the two boys sat in the doorway, and watched that night's dreams going down from Vraidex to their allotted work in the world of visionary men, to whom these dreams were passing in the form of incredible white vapors. Sitting thus, the lads fell to talking of this and the other, and Manuel found that Niafer was a pagan of the old faith: and this, said Manuel, was an excellent thing.

"For when we have achieved our adventure," says Manuel, "and must fight against each other for the Count's daughter, I shall certainly kill you, dear Niafer. Now if you were a Christian, and died thus unholily in trying to murder me, you would have to go thereafter to the unquenchable flames of Purgatory or to even hotter flames: but among the pagans all that die valiantly in battle go straight to the pagan paradise. Yes, yes, your abominable religion is a great comfort to me."

"It is a comfort to me also, Manuel. But as a Christian, you ought not to have any kind words for heathenry."

"Ah, but," says Manuel, "while my mother Dorothy of the White Arms was the most zealous sort of Christian, my father, you must know, was not a communicant."

"Who was your father, Manuel?"

"No less a person than the Swimmer, Oriander, who is in turn the son of Mimir."

"Ah, to be sure! and who is Mimir?"

"Well, Niafer, that is a thing not very generally known, but he is famed for his wise head."

"And, Manuel, who, while we speak of it, is Oriander?"

Said Manuel:

"Oh, out of the void and the darkness that is peopled by Mimir's brood, from the ultimate silent fastness of the desolate deep-sea gloom, and the peace of that ageless gloom, blind Oriander came, from Mimir, to be at war with the sea and to jeer at the sea's desire. When tempests are seething and roaring from the Æsir's inverted bowl all seamen have heard his shouting and the cry that his

mirth sends up: when the rim of the sea tilts up,
and the world's roof wavers down, his face gleams
white where distraught waves smite the Swimmer
they may not tire. No eyes were allotted this
Swimmer, but in blindness, with ceaseless jeers, he
battles till time be done with, and the love-songs
of earth be sung, and the very last dirge be sung,
and a baffled and outworn sea begrudgingly own
Oriander alone may mock at the might of its ire."

"Truly, Manuel, that sounds like a parent to be
proud of, and not at all like a church-going parent,
and of course his blindness would account for that
squint of yours. Yes, certainly it would. So do
you tell me about this blind Oriander, and how he
came to meet your mother Dorothy of the White
Arms, as I suppose he did somewhere or other."

"Oh, no," says Manuel, "for Oriander never
leaves off swimming, and so he must stay always in
the water. So he never actually met my mother,
and she married Emmerick, who is my nominal
father. But such and such things happened."

Then Manuel told Niafer all about the circumstances of Manuel's birth in a cave, and about the
circumstances of Manuel's upbringing in and near
Rathgor: and the two boys talked on and on, while
the unborn dreams went drifting by outside, and
within, the small wrinkled old man sat listening with
a very doubtful smile, and saying never a word.

"And why is your hair cut so queerly, Manuel?"

"That, Niafer, we need not talk about, in part because it is not going to be cut that way any longer, and in part because it is time for bed."

The next morning Manuel and Niafer paid the ancient price which their host required. They left him cobbling shoes, and, still ascending, encountered no more bones, for nobody else had climbed so high. They presently came to a bridge whereon were eight spears, and the bridge was guarded by the Serpent of the West. This snake was striped with blue and gold, and wore on his head a great cap of humming-birds' feathers.

Manuel half drew his sword to attack this serpentine design, with which Miramon Lluagor makes sleeping terrible for the red tribes that hunt and fish behind the Hesperides. But Manuel looked at Niafer.

And Niafer displayed a drolly marked small turtle, saying, "Maskanako, do you not recognize Tulapin, the turtle that never lies?"

The serpent howled, as though a thousand dogs had been kicked simultaneously, and the serpent fled.

"Why, snip, did he do that?" asked Manuel, smiling sleepily and gravely, as for the third time he found that his charmed sword Flamberge was unneeded.

"Truly, Manuel, nobody knows why this serpent

dreads the turtle: but our concern is less with the cause than with the effect. Meanwhile, those eight spears are not to be touched on any account."

"Is what you have a quite ordinary turtle?" asked Manuel, meekly.

Niafer said: "Of course it is. Where would I be getting extraordinary turtles?"

"I had not previously considered that problem," replied Manuel, "but the question is certainly unanswerable."

They then sat down to lunch, and found the bread and cheese they had purchased from the little old man that morning was turned to lumps of silver and virgin gold in Manuel's knapsack. "This is very disgusting," said Manuel, "and I do not wonder my back was near breaking." He flung away the treasure, and they lunched frugally on blackberries.

From among the entangled blackberry bushes came the glowing Serpent of the South, who is the smallest and loveliest and most poisonous of Miramon's designs. With this snake Niafer dealt curiously. Niafer employed three articles in the transaction: two of these things are not to be talked about, but the third was a little figure carved in hazel-wood.

"Certainly you are very clever," said Manuel, when they had passed this serpent. "Still, your employment of those first two articles was unprecedented, and your disposal of the carved figure absolutely embarrassed me."

"Before such danger as confronted us, Manuel, it does not pay to be squeamish," replied Niafer, "and my exorcism was good Dirgham."

And many other adventures and perils they encountered, such as if all were told would make a long and most improbable history. But they had clear favorable weather, and they won through each pinch, by one or another fraud, which Niafer evolved the instant that gullery was needed. Manuel was loud in his praises of the surprising cleverness of his flat-faced dark comrade, and protested that hourly he loved Niafer more and more: and Manuel said too that he was beginning to think more and more distastefully of the time when Niafer and Manuel would have to fight for the Count of Arnaye's daughter until one of them had killed the other.

Meanwhile the sword Flamberge stayed in its curious blue scabbard.

4.

In the Doubtful Palace

SO Manuel and Niafer came unhurt to the top of the gray mountain called Vraidex, and to the doubtful palace of Miramon Lluagor. Gongs, slowly struck, were sounding as if in languid dispute among themselves, when the two lads came across a small level plain where grass was interspersed with white clover. Here and there stood wicked looking dwarf trees with violet and yellow foliage. The doubtful palace before the circumspectly advancing boys appeared to be constructed of black and gold lacquer, and it was decorated with the figures of butterflies and tortoises and swans.

This day being a Thursday, Manuel and Niafer entered unchallenged through gates of horn and ivory; and came into a red corridor in which five gray beasts, like large hairless cats, were casting dice: these animals grinned and licked their lips as the boys passed deeper into the doubtful palace.

In the centre of the palace Miramon had set like a tower one of the tusks of Behemoth: the tusk was hollowed out into five large rooms, and in the inmost room, under a canopy with green tassels, they found the wizard.

"Come forth, and die now, Miramon Lluagor!" shouts Manuel, brandishing his sword, for which at last employment was promised here.

And the wizard drew closer about him his old threadbare dressing-gown, and desisted from his enchantments, and put aside a small unfinished design, which scuttled into the fireplace, whimpering. And Manuel perceived that this wizard had the appearance of the mild-mannered stranger who had given Manuel the charmed sword.

"Ah, yes, it was good of you to come so soon," says Miramon Lluagor, rearing back his head, and half closing his gentle and sombre eyes, as the wizard looked at them down the sides of what little nose he had: "yes, and your young friend, too, is very welcome. But you boys must be quite worn out, after toiling up this mountain, so do you sit down and have a cup of wine before I surrender my dear wife."

Says Manuel, sternly, "But what is the meaning of all this?"

"The meaning and the upshot, clearly," replied the wizard, "is that, since you have the charmed sword Flamberge, and since the wearer of Flamberge is irresistible, it would be nonsense for me to oppose you."

"But, Miramon, it was you who gave me the sword!"

Miramon rubbed his droll little nose for a while before speaking. "And how else was I to get conquered? For, I must tell you, Manuel, it is a law of the Léshy that a wizard cannot surrender his prey unless the wizard be conquered. I must tell you, too, that when I carried off Gisèle I acted, as I by and by discovered, rather injudiciously."

"Now, by holy Paul and Pollux! I do not understand this at all, Miramon."

"Why, Manuel, you must know she was a very charming girl, and in appearance just the type that I had always fancied for a wife. But perhaps it is not wise to be guided entirely by appearances. For I find now that she has a strong will in her white bosom, and a tireless tongue in her glittering head, and I do not equally admire all four of these possessions."

"Still, Miramon, if only a few months back your love was so great as to lead you into abducting her—"

The wizard said gravely:

"Love, as I think, is an instant's fusing of shadow and substance. They that aspire to possess love utterly fall into folly. This is forbidden: you cannot. The lover, beholding that fusing move as a golden-hued goddess, accessible, kindly and priceless, wooes and ill-fatedly wins all the substance. The golden-hued shadow dims in the dawn of his married life, dulled with content, and the shadow vanishes. So there remains, for the puzzled husband's embracing, flesh which is fair and dear, no doubt, yet is flesh such as his; and talking and talking and talking; and kisses in all ways desirable. Love, of a sort, too remains, but hardly the love that was yesterday's."

Now the unfinished design came out of the fireplace, and climbed up Miramon's leg, still faintly whimpering. He looked at it meditatively, then twisted off the creature's head and dropped the fragments into his waste-basket.

Miramon sighed. He said:

"This is the cry of all husbands that now are or may be hereafter,—'What has become of the girl that I married? and how should I rightly deal with this woman whom somehow time has involved in my doings? Love, of a sort, now I have for her, but not the love that was yesterday's—' "

While Miramon spoke thus, the two lads were looking at each other blankly: for they were young, and their understanding of this matter was as yet withheld.

Then said Miramon:

"Yes, he is wiser that shelters his longing from any such surfeit. Yes, he is wiser that knows the shadow makes lovely the substance, wisely regarding the ways of that irresponsible shadow which, if you grasp at it, flees, and, when you avoid it, will follow, gilding all life with its glory, and keeping always one woman young and most fair and most wise, and unwon; and keeping you always never contented, but armed with a self-respect that no husband manages quite to retain in the face of being contented. No, for love is an instant's fusing of shadow and substance, fused for that instant only, whereafter the lover may harvest pleasure from either alone, but hardly from these two united."

"Well," Manuel conceded, "all this may be true; but I never quite understood hexameters, and so I could not ever see the good of talking in them."

"Ah, but I always do that, Manuel, when I am deeply affected. It is, I suppose, the poetry in my nature welling to the surface the moment that inhibitions are removed, for when I think about the impending severance from my dear wife I more or less lose control of myself— You see, she takes an active interest in my work, and that does not do with a creative artist in any line. Oh, dear me, no, not for a moment!" says Miramon, forlornly.

"But how can that be?" Niafer asked him.

"As all persons know, I design the dreams of men. Now Gisèle asserts that people have enough

trouble in real life, without having to go to sleep to
look for it—"

"Certainly that is true," says Niafer.

"So she permits me only to design bright
optimistic dreams and edifying dreams and glad
dreams.   She says you must give tired persons what
they most need; and is emphatic about the importance of everybody's sleeping in a wholesome atmosphere.   So I have not been permitted to design a
fine nightmare or a creditable terror—nothing
morbid or blood-freezing, no sea-serpents or krakens
or hippogriffs, nor anything that gives me a really
free hand,—for months and months: and my art
suffers.   Then, as for other dreams, of a more
roguish nature—"

"What sort of dreams can you be talking about,
I wonder, Miramon?"

The wizard described what he meant.   "Now
such dreams also she has quite forbidden," he
added, with a sigh.

"I see," said Manuel: "and now I think of it, it
is true that I have not had a dream of that sort for
quite a while."

"No man anywhere is allowed to have that sort
of dream in these degenerate nights, no man anywhere in the whole world.   And here again my art
suffers, for my designs in this line were always
especially vivid and effective, and pleased the most

rigid. Then, too, Gisèle is always doing and telling
me things for my own good— In fine, my lads, my
wife takes such a flattering interest in all my con-
cerns that the one way out for any human wizard
was to contrive her rescue from my clutches," said
Miramon, fretfully. "It is difficult to explain to
you, Manuel, just now, but after you have been
married to Gisèle for a while you will comprehend
without any explaining."

"Now, Miramon, I marvel to see a great wizard
controlled by a woman who is in his power, and
who can, after all, do nothing but talk."

Miramon for some while considered Manuel
rather helplessly. "Unmarried men do wonder
about that," said Miramon. "At all events, I will
summon her, and you can explain how you have
conquered me, and then you can take her away and
marry her yourself, and Heaven help you!"

"But shall I explain that it was you who gave
me the resistless sword?"

"No, Manuel: no, you should be candid within
more rational limits. For you are now a famous
champion, that has crowned with victory a righteous
cause for which many stalwart knights and gallant
gentlemen have made the supreme sacrifice, because
they knew that in the end the right must conquer.
Your success thus represents the working out of a
great moral principle, and to explain the practical

minutiæ of these august processes is not always
quite respectable. Besides, if Gisèle thought I
wished to get rid of her she would most certainly
resort to comments of which I prefer not to think."

But now into the room came the wizard's wife,
Gisèle.

"She is certainly rather pretty," said Niafer, to
Manuel.

Said Manuel, rapturously: "She is the finest
and loveliest creature that I have ever seen. Beholding her unequalled beauty, I know that here
are all the dreams of yesterday fulfilled. I recollect, too, my songs of yesterday, which I was used
to sing to my pigs, about my love for a far princess
who was 'white as a lily, more red than roses, and
resplendent as rubies of the Orient,' for here I find
my old songs to be applicable, if rather inadequate.
And by this shabby wizard's failure to appreciate
such unequalled beauty I am amazed."

"Oh, as to that, I have my suspicions," Niafer replied. "And now she is about to speak I believe
she will justify these suspicions, for Madame Gisèle
is in no placid frame of mind."

"What is this nonsense," says the proud shining
lady, to Miramon Lluagor, "that I hear about your
having been conquered?"

"Alas, my love, it is perfectly true. This champion has, in some inexplicable way, come by the

magic weapon Flamberge which is the one weapon wherewith I can be conquered. So I have yielded to him, and he is about, I think, to sever my head from my body."

The beautiful girl was indignant, because she had recognized that, wizard or no, there is small difference in husbands after the first month or two; and with Miramon tolerably well trained, she had no intention of changing him for another husband. Therefore Gisèle inquired, "And what about me?" in a tone that foreboded turmoil.

The wizard rubbed his hands, uncomfortably. "My dear, I am of course quite powerless before Flamberge. Inasmuch as your rescue appears to have been effected in accordance with every rule in these matters, and the victorious champion is resolute to requite my evil-doing and to restore you to your grieving parents, I am afraid there is nothing I can well do about it."

"Do you look me in the eye, Miramon Lluagor!" says the Lady Gisèle. The wizard obeyed, with a placating smile. "Yes, you have been up to something," she said, "and Heaven only knows what, though of course it does not really matter."

Madame Gisèle then looked at Manuel. "So, you are the champion that has come to rescue me!" she said, unhastily, as her big sapphire eyes appraised him over her great fan of gaily colored feathers, and as Manuel somehow began to fidget.

Gisèle looked last of all at Niafer. "I must say you have been long enough in coming," observed Gisèle.

"It took me two days, madame, to find and catch a turtle," Niafer replied, "and that delayed me."

"Oh, you have always some tale or other, trust you for that, but it is better late than never. Come, Niafer, and do you know anything about this gawky, ragtag, yellow-haired young champion?"

"Yes, madame, he formerly lived in attendance upon the miller's pigs, down Rathgor way, and I have seen him hanging about the kitchen at Arnaye."

Gisèle turned toward the wizard, with her thin gold chains and the innumerable brilliancies of her jewels flashing no more brightly than flashed the sapphire of her eyes. "There!" she said, terribly: "and you were going to surrender me to a swine-herd, with half the hair chopped from his head, and with the shirt sticking out of both his ragged elbows!"

"My dearest, irrespective of tonsorial tastes, and disregarding all sartorial niceties, and swineherd or not, he holds the magic sword Flamberge, before which all my powers are nothing."

"But that is easily settled. Have men no sense whatever! Boy, do you give me that sword, before you hurt yourself fiddling with it, and let us have an end of this nonsense."

Thus the proud lady spoke, and for a while the victorious champion regarded her with very youthful looking, hurt eyes. But he was not routed.

"Madame Gisèle," replied Manuel, "gawky and poorly clad and young as I may be, so long as I retain this sword I am master of you all and of the future too. Yielding it, I yield everything my elders have taught me to prize, for my grave elders have taught me that much wealth and broad lands and a lovely wife are finer things to ward than a parcel of pigs. So, if I yield at all, I must first bargain and get my price for yielding."

He turned now from Gisèle to Niafer. "Dear snip," said Manuel, "you too must have your say in my bargaining, because from the first it has been your cleverness that has saved us, and has brought us two so high. For see, at last I have drawn Flamberge, and I stand at last at the doubtful summit of Vraidex, and I am master of the hour and of the future. I have but to sever the wicked head of this doomed wizard from his foul body, and that will be the end of him—"

"No, no," says Miramon, soothingly, "I shall merely be turned into something else, which perhaps we had better not discuss. But it will not inconvenience me in the least, so do you not hold back out of mistaken kindness to me, but instead do you smite, and take your well-earned reward."

"Either way," submitted Manuel, "I have but to strike, and I acquire much wealth and sleek farming-lands and a lovely wife, and the swineherd becomes a great nobleman. But it is you, Niafer, who have won all these things for me with your cleverness, and to me it seems that these wonderful rewards are less wonderful than my dear comrade."

"But you too are very wonderful," said Niafer, loyally.

Says Manuel, smiling sadly: "I am not so wonderful but that in the hour of my triumph I am frightened by my own littleness. Look you, Niafer, I had thought I would be changed when I had become a famous champion, but for all that I stand posturing here with this long sword, and am master of the hour and of the future, I remain the boy that last Thursday was tending pigs. I was not afraid of the terrors which beset me on my way to rescue the Count's daughter, but of the Count's daughter herself I am horribly afraid. Not for worlds would I be left alone with her. No, such fine and terrific ladies are not for swineherds, and it is another sort of wife that I desire."

"Whom then do you desire for a wife," says Niafer, "if not the loveliest and the wealthiest lady in all Rathgor and Lower Targamon?"

"Why, I desire the cleverest and dearest and most wonderful creature in all the world," says Manuel, —"whom I recollect seeing some six weeks ago when I was in the kitchen at Arnaye."

"Ah, ah! it might be arranged, then. But who is this marvelous woman?"

Manuel said, "You are that woman, Niafer."

Niafer replied nothing, but Niafer smiled. Niafer raised one shoulder a little, rubbing it against Manuel's broad chest, but Niafer still kept silence. So the two young people regarded each other for a while, not speaking, and to every appearance not valuing Miramon Lluagor and his encompassing enchantments at a straw's worth, nor valuing anything save each other.

"All things are changed for me," says Manuel, presently, in a hushed voice, "and for the rest of time I live in a world wherein Niafer differs from all other persons."

"My dearest," Niafer replied, "there is no sparkling queen nor polished princess anywhere but the woman's heart in her would be jumping with joy to have you looking at her twice, and I am only a servant girl!"

"But certainly," said the rasping voice of Gisèle, "Niafer is my suitably disguised heathen waiting-woman, to whom my husband sent a dream some while ago, with instructions to join me here, so that

I might have somebody to look after my things. So, Niafer, since you were fetched to wait on me, do you stop pawing at that young pig-tender, and tell me what is this I hear about your remarkable cleverness."

Instead, it was Manuel who proudly told of the shrewd devices through which Niafer had passed the serpents and the other terrors of sleep. And the while that the tall boy was boasting, Miramon Lluagor smiled, and Gisèle looked very hard at Niafer: for Miramon and his wife both knew that the cleverness of Niafer was as far to seek as her good looks, and that the dream which Miramon had sent had carefully instructed Niafer as to these devices.

"Therefore, Madame Gisèle," says Manuel, in conclusion, "I will give you Flamberge, and Miramon and Vraidex, and all the rest of earth to boot, in exchange for the most wonderful and clever woman in the world."

And with a flourish, Manuel handed over the charmed sword Flamberge to the Count's lovely daughter, and he took the hand of the swart, flat-faced servant girl.

"Come now," says Miramon, in a sad flurry, "this is an imposing performance. I need not say it arouses in me the most delightful sort of surprise and all other appropriate emotions. But as touches your own interests, Manuel, do you think your behavior is quite sensible?"

Tall Manuel looked down upon him with a sort of scornful pity. "Yes, Miramon: for I am Manuel, and I follow after my own thinking and my own desire. Of course it is very fine of me to be renouncing so much wealth and power for the sake of my wonderful dear Niafer: but she is well worth the sacrifice, and, besides, she is witnessing all this magnanimity, and cannot well fail to be impressed."

Niafer was of course reflecting: "This is very foolish and dear of him, and I shall be compelled, in mere decency, to pretend to corresponding lunacies for the first month or so of our marriage. After that, I hope, we will settle down to some more reasonable way of living."

Meanwhile she regarded Manuel fondly, and quite as though she considered him to be displaying unusual intelligence.

But Gisèle and Miramon were looking at each other, and wondering: "What can the long-legged boy see in this stupid and plain-featured girl who is years older than he? or she in the young swaggering ragged fool? And how much wiser and happier is our marriage than, in any event, the average marriage!"

So did they consider the appearance of the thing,

and so came to them the staggering thought which holds together so many couples in the teeth of human nature.

Miramon, for one, was so deeply moved by this awful reflection that he patted his wife's hand. Then he sighed. "Love has conquered my designs," said Miramon, oracularly, "and the secret of a contented marriage, after all, is to pay particular attention to the wives of everybody else."

Gisèle exhorted him not to be a fool, but she spoke without acerbity, and, speaking, she squeezed his hand. She understood this potent wizard more thoroughly than she intended ever to permit him to suspect.

Whereafter Miramon wiped the heavenly bodies from the firmament, and set a miraculous rainbow there, and under its arch was enacted for the swineherd and the waiting woman such a betrothal masque of fantasies and illusions as gave full scope to the art of Miramon, and delighted everybody, but delighted Miramon in particular. The dragon that guards hidden treasure made sport for them, the naiads danced, and cherubim fluttered about singing very sweetly and asking droll conundrums. Then they feasted, with unearthly servitors to attend them, and did all else appropriate to an affiancing of deities. And when these junketings were over, Manuel said that, since it seemed he was not to be

a wealthy nobleman after all, he and Niafer must
be getting, first to the nearest priest's, and then back
to the pigs.

"I am not so sure that you can manage it," said
Miramon, "for while the ascent of Vraidex is in-
commoded by serpents, the quitting of Vraidex is
very apt to be hindered by death and fate. For I
must tell you I have a rather arbitrary brother, who
is one of those dreadful Realists, without a scrap
of æsthetic feeling, and there is no controlling him."

"Well," Manuel considered, "one cannot live forever among dreams, and death and fate must be
encountered by all men. So we can but try."

Now for a while the sombre eyes of Miramon
Lluagor appraised them, and the wizard gave a little
sigh, for he knew that these young people were
enviable and in the outcome unimportant.

So Miramon said, "Then do you go your way,
and if you do not encounter the author and de-
stroyer of us all it will be well for you, and if you
do encounter him that too will be well in that it is
his wish."

"I neither seek nor avoid him," Manuel replied.
"I only know that I must follow after my own
thinking, and after a desire which is not to be
satisfied with dreams, even though they be"—the
boy appeared to search for a comparison, then,

smiling, said,—"as resplendent as rubies of the Orient."

Thereafter Manuel bid farewell to Miramon and Miramon's fine wife, and Manuel descended from marvelous Vraidex with his plain-featured Niafer, quite contentedly. For happiness went with them, if for no great way.

5.

The Eternal Ambuscade

MANUEL and Niafer came down from Vraidex without hindrance. There was no happier nor more devoted lover anywhere than young Manuel.

"For we will be married out of hand, dear snip," he says, "and you will help me to discharge my geas, and afterward we will travel everywhither and into the last limits of earth, so that we may see the ends of this world and may judge them."

"Perhaps we had better wait until next spring, when the roads will be better, Manuel, but certainly we will be married out of hand."

In earnest of this, Niafer permitted Manuel to kiss her again, and young Manuel said, for the twenty-second time, "There is nowhere any happiness like my happiness, nor any love like my love."

Thus speaking, and thus disporting themselves, they came leisurely to the base of the gray mountain and to the old maple-trees, under which they found two persons waiting. One was a tall man mounted on a white horse, and leading a riderless black horse. His hat was pulled down about his head so that his face could not be clearly seen.

Now the companion that was with him had the appearance of a bare-headed youngster, with dark red hair, and his face too was hidden as he sat by the roadway trimming his long finger-nails with a small green-handled knife.

"Hail, friends," said Manuel, "and for whom are you waiting here?"

"I wait for one to ride on this black horse of mine," replied the mounted stranger. "It was decreed that the first person who passed this way must be his rider, but you two come abreast. So do you choose between you which one rides."

"Well, but it is a fine steed surely," Manuel said, "and a steed fit for Charlemagne or Hector or any of the famous champions of the old time."

"Each one of them has ridden upon this black horse of mine," replied the stranger.

Niafer said, "I am frightened." And above them a furtive wind began to rustle in the torn, discolored maple-leaves.

"—For it is a fine steed and an old steed," the stranger went on, "and a tireless steed that bears all away. It has the fault, some say, that its riders do not return, but there is no pleasing everybody."

"Friend," Manuel said, in a changed voice, "who are you, and what is your name?"

"I am brother to Miramon Lluagor, lord of the nine sleeps, but I am lord of another kind of sleeping; and as for my name, it is the name that is in your thoughts, and the name which most troubles you, and the name which you think about most often."

There was silence. Manuel worked his lips foolishly. "I wish we had not walked abreast," he said. "I would we had remained among the bright dreams."

"All persons voice some regret or another at meeting me. And it does not ever matter."

"But if there were no choosing in the affair, I could make shift to endure it, either way. Now one of us, you tell me, must depart with you. If I say, 'Let Niafer be that one,' I must always recall that saying with self-loathing."

"But I too say it!" Niafer was petting him and trembling.

"Besides," observed the rider of the white horse, "you have a choice of sayings."

"The other saying," Manuel replied, "I cannot utter. Yet I wish I were not forced to confess this. It sounds badly. At all events, I love Niafer better than I love any other person, but I do not value Niafer's life more highly than I value my life, and it would be nonsense to say so. No, my life is very necessary to me, and there is a geas upon me to make a figure in this world before I leave it."

"My dearest," says Niafer, "you have chosen wisely."

The veiled horseman said nothing at all. But he took off his hat, and the beholders shuddered. The kinship to Miramon was apparent, you could see the resemblance, but they had never seen in Miramon Lluagor's face what they saw here.

Then Niafer bade farewell to Manuel with pitiable whispered words. They kissed. Thereafter Manuel, very sick and desperate looking, did what was requisite. So Niafer went away with Grandfather Death, in Manuel's stead.

"My heart cracks in me now," says Manuel, forlornly considering his hands, "but better she than I. Still, this is a poor beginning in life, for yesterday great wealth and to-day great love was within my reach, and now I have lost both."

"But you did not go the right way about to win success in anything," says the remaining stranger.

And now this other stranger arose from the trimming of his long finger-nails; and you could see this was a tall, lean youngster (though not so tall as Manuel, and nothing like so stalwart), with ruddy cheeks, wide-set brown eyes, and crinkling, rather dark red hair.

Then Manuel rubbed his wet hands as clean as might be, and this boy walked on a little way with

Manuel, talking of that which had been and of
some things which were to be. And Manuel said,
"Now assuredly, Horvendile, since that is your
name, such talking is insane talking, and no comfort whatever to me in my grief at losing Niafer."

"This is but the beginning of your losses, Manuel, for I think that a little by a little you will
lose everything which is desirable, until you shall
have remaining at the last only a satiation and a
weariness and an uneasy loathing of all that the
human wisdom of your elders shall have induced
you to procure."

"But, Horvendile, can anybody foretell the
future? Or can it be that Miramon spoke seriously
in saying that fate also was enleagued to forbid
the leaving of this mountain?"

"No, Manuel, I do not say that I am fate nor
any of the Léshy, but rather it seems to me that
I am insane. So perhaps the less attention you pay
to my talking the better. For I must tell you that
this wasted country side, this mountain, this road,
and these old maples, and that rock yonder, appear
to me to be things I have imagined: and that you,
and the Niafer whom you have just disposed of so
untidily, and Miramon and his fair shrew, and all
of you, appear to me to be persons I have imagined:
and all the living in this world appears to me to be
only a notion of mine."

"Why, then, certainly I would say, or rather, I would think it unnecessary to say, that you are insane."

"You speak without hesitation, and it is through your ability to settle such whimseys out of hand that you will yet win, it may be, to success."

"Yes, but," asked Manuel, slowly, "what is success?"

"In your deep mind, I think, that question is already answered."

"Undoubtedly I have my notion, but it was about your notion I was asking."

Horvendile looked grave, and yet whimsical too. "Why, I have heard somewhere," says he, "that at its uttermost this success is but the strivings of an ape reft of his tail, and grown rusty at climbing, who yet feels himself to be a symbol and the frail representative of Omnipotence in a place that is not home."

Manuel appeared to reserve judgment. "How does the successful ape employ himself, in these not quite friendly places?"

"He strives blunderingly, from mystery to mystery, with pathetic makeshifts, not understanding anything, greedy in all desires, and honeycombed with poltroonery, and yet ready to give all, and to die fighting for the sake of that undemonstrable idea, about his being Heaven's vicar and heir."

Manuel shook his small bright head. "You use too many long words. But so far as I can understand you, that is not the sort of success I want. No, I am Manuel, and I must follow after my own thinking and my own desire, without considering other people and their notions of success."

"As for denying yourself consideration for other people, I am of the opinion, after witnessing your recent disposal of your sweetheart, that you are already tolerably expert in that sort of abnegation."

"Hah, but you do not know what is seething here," replied Manuel, smiting his broad chest. "And I shall not tell you of it, Horvendile, since you are not fate nor any of the Léshy, to give me my desire."

"What would be your desire?"

"My wish would be for me always to obtain whatever I may wish for. Yes, Horvendile, I have often wondered why, in the old legends, when three wishes were being offered, nobody ever made that sensible and economical wish the first of all."

"What need is there to trouble the Léshy about that foolish wish when it is always possible, at a paid price, to obtain whatever one desires? You have but to go about it in this way." And Horvendile told Manuel a queer and dangerous thing. Then Horvendile said sadly: "So much knowledge I can deny nobody at Michaelmas. But I must tell you the price also, and it is that with the achieving of each desire you will perceive its worth."

Thus speaking, Horvendile parted the thicket beside the roadway. A beautiful dusk-colored woman waited there, in a green-blue robe, and on her head was a blue coronet surmounted with green feathers: she carried a vase. Horvendile stepped forward, and the thicket closed behind him, concealing Horvendile and this woman.

Manuel, looking puzzled, went on a little way, and when he was assured of being alone he flung himself face downward and wept. The reason of this was, they relate, that young Manuel had loved Niafer as he could love nobody else. Then he arose, and went toward the pool of Haranton, on his way homeward, after having failed in everything.

6.

Economics of Math

WHAT forthwith happened at the pool of Haranton is not nicely adapted to exact description, but it was sufficiently curious to give Manuel's thoughts a new turn, although it did not seem, even so, to make them happy thoughts. Certainly it was not with any appearance of merriment that Manuel returned to his sister Math, who was the miller's wife.

"And wherever have you been all this week?" says Math, "with the pigs rooting all over creation, and with that man of mine forever flinging your worthlessness in my face, and with that red-haired Suskind coming out of the twilight a-seeking after you every evening and pestering me with her soft lamentations? And for the matter of that, whatever are you glooming over?"

"I have cause, and cause to spare."

Manuel told her of his adventures upon Vraidex, and Math said that showed what came of neglecting his proper business, which was attendance on her husband's pigs. Manuel then told her of what had just befallen by the pool of Haranton.

Math nodded. "Take shame to yourself, young rascal, with your Niafer hardly settled down in paradise, and with your Suskind wailing for you in the twilight! But that would be Alianora the Unattainable Princess. Thus she comes across the Bay of Biscay, traveling from the far land of Provence, in, they say, the appearance of a swan: and thus she bathes in the pool wherein strange dreams engender: and thus she slips into the robe of the Apsarasas when it is high time to be leaving such impudent knaves as you have proved yourself to be."

"Yes, yes! a shift made all of shining white feathers, Sister. Here is a feather that was broken from it as I clutched at her."

Math turned the feather in her hand. "Now to be sure! and did you ever see the like of it! Still, a broken feather is no good to anybody, and, as I have told you any number of times, I cannot have trash littering up my kitchen."

So Math dropped this shining white feather into the fire, on which she was warming over a pot of soup for Manuel's dinner, and they watched this feather burn.

Manuel says, sighing, "Even so my days consume, and my youth goes out of me, in a land wherein Suskind whispers of uncomfortable things, and wherein there are no maids so clever and dear as Niafer, nor so lovely as Alianora."

Math said: "I never held with speaking ill of the dead. So may luck and fair words go with your Niafer in her pagan paradise. Of your Suskind too"—Math crossed herself—"the less said the better. But as for your Alianora, no really nice girl would be flying in the face of heaven and showing her ankles to five nations, and bathing, on a Monday too, in places where almost anybody might come along. It is not proper, and I wonder at her parents."

"But, Sister, she is a princess!"

"Just so: therefore I burned the feather, because it is not wholesome for persons of our station in life to be robbing princesses of anything, though it be only of a feather."

"Sister, that is the truth! It is not right to rob anybody of anything, and this would appear to make another bond upon me and another obligation to be discharged, because in taking that feather I have taken what did not belong to me."

"Boy, do not think you are fooling me, for when your face gets that look on it I know you are considering some nonsense over and above the nonsense you are talking. However, from your description of the affair, I do not doubt that gallivanting, stark-naked princess thought you were for taking what did not belong to you. Therefore I burned the feather, lest it be recognized and bring you to the gallows or to a worse place. So why did you not scrape your feet before coming into my clean kitchen? and how many times do you expect me to speak to you about that?"

Manuel said nothing. But he seemed to meditate over something that puzzled him. In the upshot he went into the miller's chicken-yard, and caught a goose, and plucked from its wing a feather.

Then Manuel put on his Sunday clothes.

"Far too good for you to be traveling in," said Math.

Manuel looked down at his half-sister, and once or twice he blinked those shining strange eyes of his. "Sister, if I had been properly dressed when I was master of the doubtful palace, the Lady Gisèle would have taken me quite seriously. I have been thinking about her observations as to my elbows."

"The coat does not make the man," replied Math piously.

"It is your belief in any such saying that has made a miller's wife of you, and will keep you a miller's wife until the end of time. Now I learned better from my misadventures upon Vraidex, and from my talking with that insane Horvendile about the things which have been and some things which are to be."

Math, who was a wise woman, said queerly, "I

perceive that you are letting your hair grow."

Manuel said, "Yes."

"Boy, fast and loose is a mischancy game to play."

"And being born, also, is a most hazardous speculation, Sister, yet we perforce risk all upon that cast."

"Now you talk stuff and nonsense—"

"Yes, Sister, but I begin to suspect that the right sort of stuff and nonsense is not unremunerative. I may be wrong, but I shall afford my notion a testing."

"And after what shiftless idiocy will you be chasing now, to neglect your work?"

"Why, as always, Sister, I must follow my own thinking and my own desire," says Manuel, lordlily, "and both of these are for a flight above pigs."

Thereafter Manuel kissed Math, and, again without taking leave of Suskind in the twilight or of anyone else, he set forth for the far land of Provence.

7.

The Crown of Wisdom

SO did it come about that as King Helmas rode a-hunting in Nevet under the Hunter's Moon he came upon a gigantic and florid young fellow, who was very decently clad in black, and had a queer droop to his left eye, and who appeared to be wandering at adventure in the autumn woods: and the King remembered what had been foretold.

Says King Helmas to Manuel the swineherd, "What is that I see in your pocket wrapped in red silk?"

"It is a feather, King, wrapped in a bit of my sister's best petticoat."

"Now, glory be to your dark magics, friend, and at what price will you sell me that feather?"

"But a feather is no use to anybody, King, for, as you see, it is a quite ordinary feather."

"Come, come!" the King says, shrewdly, "do people anywhere wrap ordinary feathers in red silk? Friend, do not think to deceive King Helmas of Albania, or it will be the worse for you. I perfectly recognize that shining white feather as the feather which was moulted in this forest by the

Zhar-Ptitza Bird, in the old time before my grand-fathers came into this country. For it was fore-told that such a young sorcerer as you would bring to me, who have long been the silliest King that ever reigned over the Peohtes, this feather which confers upon its owner perfect wisdom: and for you to dispute the prophecy would be blasphemous."

"I do not dispute your silliness, King Helmas, nor do I dispute anybody's prophecies in a world wherein nothing is certain."

"One thing at least is certain," remarked King Helmas, frowning uglily, "and it is that among the Peohtes all persons who dispute our prophecies are burned at the stake."

Manuel shivered slightly, and said: "It seems to me a quite ordinary feather: but your prophets —most deservedly, no doubt—are in higher repute for wisdom than I am, and burning is a discom-fortable death. So I recall what a madman told me, and, since you are assured that this is the Zhar-Ptitza's feather, I will sell it to you for ten sequins."

King Helmas shook a disapproving face. "That will not do at all, and your price is out of reason, because it was foretold that for this feather you would ask ten thousand sequins."

"Well, I am particularly desirous not to appear irreligious now that I have become a young sorcerer.

So you may have the feather at your own price, rather than let the prophecies remain unfulfilled."

Then Manuel rode pillion with a king who was unwilling to let Manuel out of his sight, and they went thus to Brunbelois and to the vine-covered palace of King Helmas. They came to two doors with pointed arches, set side by side, the smaller being for foot passengers, and the other for horsemen. Above was an equestrian statue in a niche, and a great painted window with traceries of hearts and thistles.

They entered the larger door, and that afternoon twelve heralds, in bright red tabards that were embroidered with golden thistles, rode out of this door, to proclaim the fulfilment of the prophecy as to the Zhar-Ptitza's feather, and that afternoon the priests of the Peohtes gave thanks in all their curious underground temples. The common people, who had for the last score of years taken shame to themselves for living under such a foolish king, embraced one another, and danced, and sang patriotic songs at every street-corner: the Lower Council met, and voted that out of deference to his majesty All Fools' Day should be stricken from the calendar: and Queen Pressina (one of the water folk) declared there were two ways of looking at everything, the while that she burned a quantity of

private papers. Then at night were fireworks, the
King made a speech, and to Manuel was paid ten
thousand sequins.

Thereafter Manuel abode for a month at the
court of King Helmas, noting whatever to this side
and to that side seemed most notable. Manuel was
well liked by the nobility, and when the barons and
the fine ladies assembled in the evening for pavanes
and branles and pazzamenos nobody danced more
statelily than Messire Manuel. He had a quiet way
with the ladies, and with the barons a way of
simplicity which was vastly admired in a sorcerer so
potent that his magic had secured the long sought
Zhar-Ptitza's feather. "But the most learned," as
King Helmas justly said, "are always the most
modest."

Helmas now wore the feather from the wing of
the miller's goose affixed to the front of Helmas'
second best crown, because that was the one he
used to give judgments in. And when it was noised
abroad that King Helmas had the Zhar-Ptitza's
feather, the Peohtes came gladly to be judged, and
the neighboring kings began to submit to him their
more difficult cases, and all his judgings were re-
ceived with reverence, because everybody knew that
King Helmas' wisdom was now infallible, and that
to criticize his verdict as to anything was merely
to expose your own stupidity.

And now that doubt of himself had gone out of his mind, Helmas lived untroubled, and his digestion improved, and his loving-kindness was infinite, because he could not be angry with the pitiable creatures haled before him, when he considered how little able they were to distinguish between wisdom and unwisdom where Helmas was omniscient: and all his doings were merciful and just, and his people praised him.   Even the Queen conceded that, once you were accustomed to his ways, and exercised some firmness about being made a doormat of, and had it understood once for all that meals could not be kept waiting for him, she supposed there might be women worse off.

And Manuel got clay and modeled the figure of a young man which had the features and the wise look of King Helmas.

"I can see the resemblance," the King said, "but it does not half do me justice, and, besides, why have you made a young whipper-snapper of me, and mixed up my appearance with your appearance?"

"I do not know," said Manuel, "but I suppose it is because of a geas which is upon me to make myself a splendid and admirable young man in every respect, and not an old man."

"And does the sculpture satisfy you?" asks the King, smiling wisely.

"No, I like this figure well enough, now it is done, but it is not, I somehow know, the figure I desire to make. No, I must follow after my own thinking and my own desire, and wisdom is not requisite to me."

"You artists!" said the King, as people always say that. "Now I would consider that, for all the might of your sorceries, wisdom is rather clamantly requisite to you, Messire Manuel, who inform me you must soon be riding hence to find elsewhere the needful look for your figure. For thus to be riding about this world of men, in search of a shade of expression, and without even being certain of what look you are looking for, does not appear to me to be good sense."

But young Manuel replied sturdily:

"I ride to encounter what life has in store for me, who am made certain of this at least, that all high harvests which life withholds for me spring from a seed which I sow—and reap. For my geas is potent, and, late or soon, I serve my geas, and take my doom as the pay well-earned that is given as pay to me, for the figure I make in this world of men.

"This figure, foreseen and yet hidden away from me, glimpsed from afar in the light of a dream,—will I love it, once made, or will loathing awake in me after its visage is plainlier seen? No matter:

as fate says so say I, who serve my geas and gain in time such payment, at worst, as is honestly due to me, for the figure I make in this world of men.

"To its shaping I consecrate youth that is strong in me, ardently yielding youth's last least gift, who know that all grace which the gods have allotted me avails me in naught if it fails me in this. For all that a man has, that must I bring to the image I shape, that my making may live when time unmakes me and death dissevers me from the figure I make in this world of men."

To this the King rather drily replied: "There is something in what you say. But that something is, I can assure you, not wisdom."

So everyone was satisfied in Albania except Manuel, who declared that he was pleased but not contented by the image he had made in the likeness of King Helmas.

"Besides," they told him, "you look as though your mind were troubling you about something."

"In fact, I am puzzled to see a foolish person made wise in all his deeds and speeches by this wisdom being expected of him."

"But that is a cause for rejoicing, and for applauding the might of your sorceries, Messire Manuel, whereas you are plainly thinking of vexatious matters."

Manuel replied, "I think that it is not right to

rob anybody of anything, and I reflect that wisdom weighs exactly the weight of a feather."

Then Manuel went into King Helmas' chicken-yard, and caught a goose, and plucked from its wing a feather. Manuel went glitteringly now, in bro-caded hose, and with gold spurs on his heels: the figure which he had made in the likeness of King Helmas was packed in an expensive knapsack of ornamented leather, and tall shining Manuel rode on a tall dappled horse when he departed south-ward, for Manuel nowadays had money to spare.

NOW Manuel takes ship across the fretful Bay of Biscay, traveling always toward Provence and Alianora, whom people called the Unattainable Princess. Oriander the Swimmer followed this ship, they say, but he attempted to do Manuel no hurt for that turn.

So Manuel of the high head comes into the country of wicked King Ferdinand, and, toward All-Hallows, they bring a stupendous florid young man to the King in the torture-chamber. King Ferdinand was not idle at the moment, and he looked up good-temperedly enough from his employment: but almost instantly his merry face was overcast.

"Dear me!" says Ferdinand, as he dropped his white hot pincers sizzlingly into a jar of water, "and I had hoped you would not be bothering me for a good ten years!"

"Now if I bother you at all it is against my will," declared Manuel, very politely, "nor do I willingly intrude upon you here, for, without criticizing anybody's domestic arrangements, there are one or two

things that I do not fancy the looks of in this torture-chamber."

"That is as it may be.   In the mean time, what
is that I see in your pocket wrapped in red silk?"

"It is a feather, King, wrapped in a bit of my
sister's best petticoat."

Then Ferdinand sighed, and he arose from his
interesting experiments with what was left of the
Marquess de Henestrosa, to whom the King had
taken a sudden dislike that morning.

"Tut, tut!" said Ferdinand: "yet, after all, I have
had a brave time of it, with my enormities and my
iniquities, and it is not as though there were nothing
to look back on! So at what price will you sell
me that feather?"

"But surely a feather is no use to anybody, King,
for does it not seem to you a quite ordinary
feather?"

"Come!" says King Ferdinand, as he washed his
hands, "do people anywhere wrap ordinary feathers
in red silk? You squinting rascal, do not think to
swindle me out of eternal bliss by any such foolish
talk! I perfectly recognize that feather as the
feather which Milcah plucked from the left pinion
of the Archangel Oriphiel when the sons of God
were on more intricate and scandalous terms with
the daughters of men than are permitted nowadays."

"Well, sir," replied Manuel, "you may be right
in a world wherein nothing is certain. At all
events, I have deduced, from one or two things in
this torture-chamber, that it is better not to argue
with King Ferdinand."

"How can I help being right, when it was foretold long ago that such a divine emissary as you
would bring this very holy relic to turn me from my
sins and make a saint of me?" says Ferdinand,
peevishly.

"It appears to me a quite ordinary feather, King:
but I recall what a madman told me, and I do not
dispute that your prophets are wiser than I, for
I have been a divine emissary for only a short
while."

"Do you name your price for this feather, then!"

"I think it would be more respectful, sir, to refer
you to the prophets, for I find them generous and
big-hearted creatures."

Ferdinand nodded his approval. "That is very
piously spoken, because it was prophesied that this
relic would be given me for no price at all by a
great nobleman. So I must forthwith write out for
you a count's commission, I suppose, and must
write out your grants to fertile lands and a stout
castle or two, and must date your title to these
things from yesterday."

"Certainly," said Manuel, "it would not look

well for you to be neglecting due respect to such a famous prophecy, with that bottle of ink at your elbow."

So King Ferdinand sent for the Count of Poictesme, and explained to him as between old friends how the matter stood, and that afternoon the high Count was confessed and decapitated. Poictesme being now a vacant fief, King Ferdinand ennobled Manuel, and made him Count of Poictesme.

It was true that all Poictesme was then held by the Northmen, under Duke Asmund, who denied King Ferdinand's authority with contempt, and defeated him in battle with annoying persistence: so that Manuel for the present acquired nothing but the sonorous title.

"Some terrible calamity, however," as King Ferdinand pointed out, "is sure to befall Asmund and his iniquitous followers before very long, so we need not bother about them."

"But how may I be certain of that, sir?" Manuel asked.

"Count, I am surprised at such scepticism! Is it not very explicitly stated in Holy Writ that though the wicked may flourish for a while they are presently felled like green bay-trees?"

"Yes, to be sure. So there is no doubt that your soldiers will soon conquer Duke Asmund."

"But I must not send any soldiers to fight against him, now that I am a saint, for that would not look well. It would have an irreligious appearance of prompting Heaven."

"Still, King, you are sending soldiers against the Moors—"

"Ah, but it is not your lands, Count, but my city of Ubeda, which the Moors are attacking, and to attack a saint, as you must undoubtedly understand, is a dangerous heresy which it is my duty to put down."

"Yes, to be sure. Well, well!" says Manuel, "at any rate, to be a count is something, and it is better to ward a fine name than a parcel of pigs, though it appears the pigs are the more nourishing."

In the meanwhile the King's heralds rode everywhither in fluted armor, to proclaim the fulfilment of the old prophecy as to the Archangel Oriphiel's feather. Never before was there such a hubbub in those parts, for the bells of all the churches sounded all day, and all the people ran about praying at the top of their voices, and forgiving their relatives, and kissing the girls, and blowing whistles and ringing cow-bells, because the city now harbored a relic so holy that the vilest sinner had but to touch it to be purified of iniquity.

And that day King Ferdinand dismissed the evil companions with whom he had so long rioted in

every manner of wickedness, and Ferdinand lived
henceforward as became a saint. He builded two
churches a year, and fared edifyingly on roots and
herbs; he washed the feet of three indigent persons
daily, and went in sackcloth; whenever he burned
heretics he fetched and piled up the wood himself,
so as to inconvenience nobody; and he made
prioresses and abbesses of his more intimate and
personal associates of yesterday, because he knew
that people are made holy by contact with holiness,
and that sainthood is retro-active.

Thereafter Count Manuel abode for a month at
the court of King Ferdinand, noting whatever to
this side and to that side seemed most notable.
Manuel was generally liked by the elect, and in the
evening when the court assembled for family-
prayers nobody was more devout than the Count of
Poictesme. He had a quiet way with the abbesses
and prioresses, and with the anchorites and bishops
a way of simplicity which was vastly admired in a
divine emissary. "But the particular favor of
Heaven," as King Ferdinand pointed out, "is always reserved for modest persons."

The feather from the wing of Helmas' goose
King Ferdinand had caused to be affixed to the un-
assuming skullcap with a halo of gold wire which
Ferdinand now wore in the place of a vainglorious
earthly crown; so that perpetual contiguity with

this relic might keep him in augmenting sanctity. And now that doubt of himself had gone out of his mind, Ferdinand lived untroubled, and his digestion improved on his light diet of roots and herbs, and his loving-kindness was infinite, because he could not now be angry with the pitiable creatures haled before him, when he considered what lengthy and ingenious torments awaited every one of them, either in hell or purgatory, while Ferdinand would be playing a gold harp in heaven.

So Ferdinand dealt tenderly and generously with all. Half of his subjects said that simply showed you: and the rest of them assented that indeed you might well say that, and they had often thought of it, and had wished that young people would take profit by considering such things more seriously.

And Manuel got clay and modeled a figure which had the features and the holy look of King Ferdinand.

"Yes, this young fellow you have made of mud is something like me," the King conceded, "although clay of course cannot do justice to the fine red cheeks and nose I used to have in the unregenerate days when I thought about such vanities, and, besides, it is rather more like you. Still, Count, the thing has feeling, it is wholesome, it is refreshingly free from these modern morbid considerations of anatomy, and it does you credit."

"No, King, I like this figure well enough, now
that it is done, but it is not, I somehow know, the
figure I desire to make. No, I must follow after
my own thinking and my own desires, and I do not
need holiness."

"You artists!" the King said. "But there is
more than mud upon your mind."

"In fact, I am puzzled, King, to see you made a
saint of by its being expected of you."

"But, Count, that ought to grieve nobody, so
long as I do not complain, and it is of something
graver you are thinking."

"I think, sir, that it is not right to rob anybody
of anything, and I reflect that absolute righteous-
ness is a fine feather in one's cap."

Then Manuel went into the chicken-yard behind
the red-roofed palace of King Ferdinand, and
caught a goose, and plucked from its wing a feather.
Thereafter the florid young Count of Poictesme
rode east, on a tall dappled horse, and a retinue of
six lackeys in blue and yellow liveries came canter-
ing after him, and the two foremost lackeys carried
in knapsacks, marked with a gold coronet, the
images which Dom Manuel had made. A third
lackey carried Dom Manuel's shield, whereon was
emblazoned the rampant and bridled stallion of
Poictesme, but the old arms had now a new motto.

"What means this Greek?" Dom Manuel had asked.

"*Mundus decipit,* Count," they told him, "is the old pious motto of Poictesme: it signifies that the affairs of this world are a vain fleeting show, and that terrestrial appearances are nowhere of any particular importance."

"Then your motto is green inexperience," said Manuel, "and for me to bear it would be black ingratitude."

So the writing had been changed in accordance with his instructions, and it now read *Mundus vult decipi.*

IN such estate it was that Count Manuel came, on Christmas morning, just two days after Manuel was twenty-one, into Provence. This land, reputed sorcerous, in no way displayed to him any unusual features, though it was noticeable that the King's marmoreal palace was fenced with silver pikes whereon were set the embalmed heads of young men who had wooed the Princess Alianora unsuccessfully. Manuel's lackeys did not at first like the looks of these heads, and said they were unsuitable for Christmas decorations: but Dom Manuel explained that at this season of general merriment this palisade also was mirth-provoking because (the weather being such as was virtually unprecedented in these parts) a light snow had fallen during the night, so that each head seemed to wear a nightcap.

They bring Manuel to Raymond Bérenger, Count of Provence and King of Arles, who was holding the Christmas feast in his warm hall. Raymond sat on a fine throne of carved white ivory and gold, beneath a purple canopy. And beside him, upon just such another throne, not quite so high, sat Raymond's daughter, Alianora the Unattainable Princess, in a robe of watered silk which was of seven colors and was lined with the dark fur of barbiolets. In her crown were chrysolites and amethysts: it was a wonder to note how brightly they shone, but they were not so bright as Alianora's eyes.

She stared as Manuel of the high head came through the hall, wherein the barons were seated according to their degrees. She had, they say, four reasons for remembering the impudent huge squinting yellow-haired young fellow whom she had encountered at the pool of Haranton. She blushed, and spoke with her father in the whistling and hissing language which the Apsarasas use among themselves: and her father laughed long and loud.

Says Raymond Bérenger: "Things might have fallen out much worse. Come tell me now, Count of Poictesme, what is that I see in your breast pocket wrapped in red silk?"

"It is a feather, King," replied Manuel, a little wearily, "wrapped in a bit of my sister's best petticoat."

"Ay, ay," says Raymond Bérenger, with a grin that was becoming even more benevolent, "and I need not ask what price you come expecting for that feather. None the less, you are an excellently

spoken-of young wizard of noble condition, who
have slain no doubt a reasonable number of giants
and dragons, and who have certainly turned kings
from folly and wickedness. For such fine rumors
speed before the man who has fine deeds behind
him that you do not come into my realm as a
stranger : and, I repeat, things might have fallen out
much worse."

"Now listen, all ye that hold Christmas here!"
cried Manuel. "A while back I robbed this
Princess of a feather, and the thought of it lay in
my mind more heavy than a feather, because I had
taken what did not belong to me. So a bond was
on me, and I set out toward Provence to restore to
her a feather. And such happenings befell me by
the way that at Michaelmas I brought wisdom into
one realm, and at All-Hallows I brought piety into
another realm. Now what I may be bringing into
this realm of yours at Heaven's most holy season,
Heaven only knows. To the eye it may seem a
quite ordinary feather. Yet life in the wide world,
I find, is a queerer thing than ever any swineherd
dreamed of in his wattled hut, and people everywhere are nourished by their beliefs, in a way that
the meat of pigs can nourish nobody."

Raymond Bérenger said, with a wise nod : "I
perceive what is in your heart, and I see likewise

what is in your pocket. So why do you tell me what everybody knows? Everybody knows that the robe of the Apsarasas, which is the peculiar treasure of Provence, has been ruined by the loss of a feather, so that my daughter can no longer go abroad in the appearance of a swan, because the robe is not able to work any more wonders until that feather in your pocket has been sewed back into the robe with the old incantation."

"Now, but indeed does everybody know that!" says Manuel.

"—Everybody knows, too, that my daughter has pined away with fretting after her lost ways of out-door exercise, and the healthful changes of air which she used to be having. And finally, everybody knows that, at my daughter's very sensible suggestion, I have offered my daughter's hand in marriage to him who would restore that feather, and death to every impudent young fellow who dared enter here without it, as my palace fence attests."

"Oh, oh!" says Manuel, smiling, "but seemingly it is no wholesome adventure which has come to me unsought!"

"—So, as you tell me, you came into Provence: and, as there is no need to tell me, I hope, who have still two eyes in my head, you have achieved

the adventure.   So why do you keep telling me
about matters with which I am as well acquainted
as you?"

"But, King of Arles, how do you know that this
is not an ordinary feather?"

"Count of Poictesme, do people anywhere—"

"Oh, spare me that vile bit of worldly logic, sir,
and I will concede whatever you desire!"

"Then do you stop talking such nonsense, and
give my daughter her feather!"

Manuel ascends the white throne of Alianora.
"Queer things have befallen me," said Manuel, "but
nothing more strange than this can ever happen,
than that I should be standing here with you, and
holding this small hand in mine.   You are not perhaps quite so beautiful nor so clever as Niafer.
Nevertheless, you are the Unattainable Princess,
whose loveliness recalled me from vain grieving
after Niafer, within a half-hour of Niafer's loss.
Yes, you are she whose beauty kindled a dream and
a dissatisfaction in the heart of a swineherd, to
lead him forth into the wide world, and through
the puzzling ways of the wide world, and into its
high places: so that at the last the swineherd is
standing—a-glitter in satin and gold and in rich
furs,—here at the summit of a throne; and at the
last the hand of the Unattainable Princess is in his
hand, and in his heart is misery."

The Princess said, "I do not know anything about this Niafer, who was probably no better than she should have been, nor do I know of any conceivable reason for your being miserable."

"Why, is it not the truth," asks Manuel of Alianora, speaking not very steadily, "that you are to marry the man who restores the feather of which you were robbed at the pool of Haranton, and can marry none other?"

"It is the truth," she answered, in a small frightened lovely voice, "and I no longer grieve that it is the truth, and I think it a most impolite reason for your being miserable."

Manuel laughed without ardor. "See how we live and learn! I recall now the droll credulity of a lad who watched a shining feather burned, while he sat within arm's reach thinking about cabbage soup, because his grave elders assured him that a feather could never be of any use to anybody. And that, too, after he had seen what uses may be made of an old bridle or of a duck egg or of anything! Well, but all water that is past the dam must go its way, even though it be a flood of tears—"

Here Manuel gently shrugged broad shoulders. He took out of his pocket the feather he had plucked from the wing of Ferdinand's goose.

He said: "A feather I took from you in the red autumn woods, and a feather I now restore to you, my Princess, in this white palace of yours, not asking any reward, and not claiming to be remembered by you in the gray years to come, but striving to leave no obligation undischarged and no debt unpaid. And whether in this world wherein nothing is certain, one feather is better than another feather, I do not know. It well may come about that I must straightway take a foul doom from fair lips, and that presently my head will be drying on a silver pike. Even so, one never knows: and I have learned that it is well to put all doubt of oneself quite out of mind."

He gave her the feather he had plucked from the third goose, and the trumpets sounded as a token that the quest of Alianora's feather had been fulfilled, and all the courtiers shouted in honor of Count Manuel.

Alianora looked at what was in her hand, and saw it was a goose-feather, in nothing resembling the feather which, when she had fled in maidenly embarrassment from Manuel's over-friendly advances, she had plucked from the robe of the Apsarasas, and had dropped at Manuel's feet, in order that her father might be forced to proclaim this quest, and the winning of it might be predetermined.

Then Alianora looked at Manuel. Now before her the queer unequal eyes of this big young man were bright and steadfast as altar candles. His chin was well up, and it seemed to her that this fine young fellow expected her to declare the truth, when the truth would be his death-sentence. She had no patience with his nonsense.

Says Alianora, with that lovely tranquil smile of hers: "Count Manuel has fulfilled the quest. He has restored to me the feather from the robe of the Apsarasas. I recognize it perfectly."

"Why, to be sure," says Raymond Bérenger. "Still, do you get your needle and the recipe for the old incantation, and the robe too, and make it plain to all my barons that the power of the robe is returned to it, by flying about the hall a little in the appearance of a swan. For it is better to conduct these affairs in due order and without any suspicion of irregularity."

Now matters looked ticklish for Dom Manuel, since he and Alianora knew that the robe had been spoiled, and that the addition of any number of goose-feathers was not going to turn Alianora into a swan. Yet the boy's handsome and high-colored face stayed courteously attentive to the wishes of his host, and did not change.

But Alianora said indignantly: "My father, I am surprised at you! Have you no sense of decency at all? You ought to know it is not becoming for an engaged girl to be flying about Pro-

vence in the appearance of a swan, far less among
a parcel of men who have been drinking all morning.   It is the sort of thing that leads to a girl's
being talked about."

"Now, that is true, my dear," said Raymond
Bérenger, abashed, "and the sentiment does you
credit.   So perhaps I had better suggest something
else—"

"Indeed, my father, I see exactly what you would
be suggesting.   And I believe you are right."

"I am not infallible, my dear: but still—"

"Yes, you are perfectly right: it is not well for
any married woman to be known to possess any
such robe.   There is no telling, just as you say,
what people would not be whispering about her,
nor what disgraceful tricks she would not get the
credit of playing on her husband."

"My daughter, I was only about to tell you—"

"Yes, and you put it quite unanswerably.   For
you, who have the name of being the wisest Count
that ever reigned in Provence, and the shrewdest
King that Arles has ever had, know perfectly well
how people talk, and how eager people are to talk,
and to place the very worst construction on everything: and you know, too, that husbands do not like
such talk.   Certainly I had not thought of these
things, my father, but I believe that you are right."

Raymond Bérenger stroked his thick short beard,

and said: "Now truly, my daughter, whether or
not I be wise and shrewd—though, as you say, of
course there have been persons kind enough to consider—and in petitions too— However, be that as it
may, and putting aside the fact that everybody likes
to be appreciated, I must confess I can imagine no
gift which would at this high season be more ac-
ceptable to any husband than the ashes of that
robe."

"This is a saying," Alianora here declares, "well
worthy of Raymond Bérenger: and I have often
wondered at your striking way of putting things."

"That, too, is a gift," the King-Count said, with
proper modesty, "which to some persons is given,
and to others not: so I deserve no credit for it.
But, as I was saying when you interrupted me, my
dear, it is well for youth to have its fling, because
(as I have often thought) we are young only once:
and so I have not ever criticized your jauntings
in far lands. But a husband is another pair of
sandals. A husband does not like to have his wife
flying about the tree-tops and the tall lonely moun-
tains and the low long marshes, with nobody to keep
an eye on her, and that is the truth of it. So, were
I in your place, and wise enough to listen to the old
father who loves you, and who is wiser than you,
my dear—why, now that you are about to marry, I
repeat to you with all possible earnestness, my dar-

ling, I would destroy this feather and this robe in one red fire, if only Count Manuel will agree to it. For it is he who now has power over all your possessions, and not I."

"Count Manuel," says Alianora, with that lovely tranquil smile of hers, "you perceive that my father is insistent, and it is my duty to be guided by him. I do not deny that, upon my father's advice, I am asking you to let perish a strong magic which many persons would value above a woman's pleading. But I know now"—her eyes met his, and to any young man anywhere with a heart moving in him, that which Manuel could see in the bright frightened eyes of Alianora could not but be a joy well-nigh intolerable,—"but I know now that you, who are to be my husband, and who have brought wisdom into one kingdom, and piety into another, have brought love into the third kingdom: and I perceive that this third magic is a stronger and a nobler magic than that of the Apsarasas. And it seems to me that you and I would do well to dispense with anything which is second rate."

"I am of the opinion that you are a singularly intelligent young woman," says Manuel, "and I am of the belief that it is far too early for me to be crossing my wife's wishes, in a world wherein all men are nourished by their beliefs."

All being agreed, the Yule-log was stirred up into

a blaze, which was duly fed with the goose-feather and the robe of the Apsarasas.   Thereafter the trumpets sounded a fanfare, to proclaim that Raymond Bérenger's collops were cooked and peppered, his wine casks broached, and his puddings steaming. Then the former swineherd went in to share his Christmas dinner with the King-Count's daughter, Alianora, whom people everywhere had called the Unattainable Princess.

And they relate that while Alianora and Manuel sat cosily in the hood of the fireplace and cracked walnuts, and in the pauses of their talking noted how the snow was drifting by the windows, the ghost of Niafer went restlessly about green fields beneath an ever radiant sky in the paradise of the pagans.   When the kindly great-browed warders asked her what it was she was seeking, the troubled spirit could not tell them, for Niafer had tasted Lethe, and had forgotten Dom Manuel.   Only her love for him had not been forgotten, because that love had become a part of her, and so lived on as a blind longing and as a desire that did not know its aim.   And they relate also that in Suskind's low red-pillared palace Suskind waited with an old thought for company.

PART TWO

THE BOOK OF SPENDING

TO
LOUIS UNTERMEYER.

"Often tymes herde Manuel tell of the fayrness of this Queene of *Furies* and *Gobblins* and *Hydræs,* insomuch that he was enamoured of hyr, though he neuer sawe hyr : then by his Connynge made he a Hole in the fyer, and went ouer to hyr, and when he had spoke with hyr, he shewed hyr his mynde."

10.

Alianora

THEY of Poictesme narrate that after dinner
King Raymond sent messengers to his wife,
who was spending that Christmas with their
daughter, Queen Meregrett of France, to bid Dame
Beatrice return as soon as might be convenient, so
that they might marry off their daughter Alianora
to the famous Count Manuel. They tell also how
the holiday season passed with every manner of
festivity, and how Dom Manuel got on splendidly
with his Princess, and how it appeared to onlookers
that for both of them, even for the vaguely con-
descending boy, love-making proved a very marvelous and dear pursuit.

Dom Manuel confessed, in reply to jealous ques-
tionings, that he did not think Alianora quite so
beautiful nor so clever as Niafer had been, but this,
as Manuel pointed out, was hardly a matter which
could be remedied. At all events, the Princess was
a fine-looking and intelligent girl, as Dom Manuel
freely conceded to her: and the magic of the
Apsarasas, in which she was instructing him, Dom

Manuel declared to be very interesting if you cared for that sort of thing.

The Princess humbly admitted, in reply, that of course her magic did not compare with his, since hers was powerful only over the bodies of men and beasts, whereas Dom Manuel's magic had so notably controlled the hearts and minds of kings. Still, as Alianora pointed out, she could blight corn and cattle, and raise tempests very handily, and, given time, could smite an enemy with almost any physical malady you selected. She could not kill outright to be sure, but even so, these lesser mischiefs were not despicable accomplishments in a young girl. Anyhow, she said in peroration, it was atrocious to discourage her by laughing at the best she could do.

"Ah, but come now, my dear," says Manuel, "I was only teasing. I really think your work most promising. You have but to continue. Practise, that is the thing, they say, in all the arts."

"Yes, and with you to help me—"

"No, I have graver matters to attend to than devil-mongering," says Manuel, "and a bond to lift from myself before I can lay miseries on others."

For because of the geas that was on him to make a figure in the world, Dom Manuel had unpacked his two images, and after vexedly considering them, he had fallen again to modelling in clay, and had made a third image. This image also was in the likeness of a young man, but it had the fine proud features and the loving look of Alianora.

Manuel confessed to being fairly well pleased with this figure, but even so, he did not quite recognize in it the figure he desired to make, and therefore, he said, he deduced that love was not the thing which was essential to him.

Alianora did not like the image at all.

"To have made an image of me," she considered, "would have been a very pretty compliment. But when it comes to pulling about my features, as if they did not satisfy you, and mixing them up with your features, until you have made the appearance of a young man that looks like both of us, it is not a compliment. Instead, it is the next thing but one to egotism."

"Perhaps, now I think of it, I am an egotist. At all events, I am Manuel."

"Nor, dearest," says she, "is it quite befitting that you, who are now betrothed to a princess, and who are going to be Lord of Provence and King of Arles, as soon as I can get rid of Father, should be always messing with wet mud."

"I know that very well," Manuel replied, "but, none the less, a geas is on me to honor my mother's wishes, and to make an admirable and significant figure in the world. Apart from that, though, Alianora, I repeat to you, this scheme of yours,

about poisoning your father as soon as we are
married, appears to me for various reasons ill-ad-
vised. I am in no haste to be King of Arles, and,
in fact, I am not sure that I wish to be king at all,
because my geas is more important."

"Sweetheart, I love you very much, but my love
does not blind me to the fact that, no matter what
your talents at sorcery, you are in everyday matters
a hopelessly unpractical person. Do you leave this
affair to me, and I will manage it with every regard
to appearances."

"Ah, and does one have to preserve appearances
even in such matters as parricide?"

"But certainly it looks much better for Father
to be supposed to die of indigestion. People would
be suspecting all sorts of evil of the poor dear if
it were known that his own daughter could not put
up with him. In any event, sweetheart, I am re-
solved that, since very luckily Father has no sons,
you shall be King of Arles before this new year is
out."

"No, I am Manuel: and it means more to me to
be Manuel than to be King of Arles, and Count of
Provence, and seneschal of Aix and Brignoles and
Grasse and Massilia and Draguignan and so on."

"Oh, you are breaking my heart with this neglect
of your true interests! And it is all the doing of
these three vile images, which you value more than

the old throne of Boson and Rothbold, and oceans more than you do me!"

"Come, I did not say that."

"Yes, and you think, too, a deal more about that dead heathen servant girl than you do about me, who am a princess and the heir to a kingdom."

Manuel looked at Alianora for a considerable while before speaking. "My dear, you are, as I have always told you, an unusually fine looking and intelligent girl. And yes, you are a princess, of course, though you are no longer the Unattainable Princess: that makes a difference certainly— But, over and above all this, there was never anybody like Niafer, and it would be nonsense to pretend otherwise."

The Princess said: "I wonder at myself. You are schooled in strange sorceries unknown to the Apsarasas, there is no questioning that after the miracles you wrought with Helmas and Ferdinand: even so, I too have a neat hand at magic, and it is not right for you to be treating me as though I were the dirt under your feet. And I endure it! It is that which puzzles me, it makes me wonder at myself, and my sole comfort is that, at any rate, this wonderful Niafer of yours is dead and done with."

Manuel sighed. "Yes, Niafer is dead, and these images also are dead things, and both these facts

continually trouble me.   Nothing can be done about
Niafer, I suppose, but if only I could give some
animation to these images I think the geas upon
me would be satisfied."

"Such a desire is blasphemous, Manuel, for the
Eternal Father did no more than that with His
primal sculptures in Eden."

Dom Manuel blinked his vivid blue eyes as if in
consideration.   "Well, but," he said, gravely, "but
if I am a child of God it is only natural, I think,
that I should inherit the tastes and habits of my
Father.   No, it is not blasphemous, I think, to desire to make an animated and lively figure, somewhat more admirable and significant than that of
the average man.   No, I think not.   Anyhow,
blasphemous or not, that is my need, and I must
follow after my own thinking and my own desire."

"If that desire were satisfied," asks Alianora,
rather queerly, "would you be content to settle down
to some such rational method of living as becomes
a reputable sorcerer and king?"

"I think so, for a king has no master, and he is
at liberty to travel everywhither, and to see the
ends of this world and judge them.   Yes, I think
so, in a world wherein nothing is certain."

"If I but half way believed that, I would en-
deavor to obtain Schamir, and put you to the test."

"And what in the devil is this Schamir?"

"A slip of the tongue," replied Alianora, smiling. "No, I shall have nothing to do with your idiotic mud figures, and I shall tell you nothing further."

"Come now, pettikins!" says Manuel. And he began coaxing the Princess of Provence with just such cajoleries as the big handsome boy had formerly exercised against the peasant girls of Rathgor.

"Schamir," said Alianora, at last, "is set in a signet-ring which is very well known in the country on the other side of the fire. Schamir has the appearance of a black pebble, and if, after performing the proper ceremonies, you were to touch one of these figures with it the figure would become animated."

"Well, but," says Manuel, "the difficulty is that if I attempt to pass through the fire in order to reach the country behind it, I shall be burned to a cinder, and so I have no way of obtaining this talisman."

"In order to obtain it," Alianora told him, "one must hard-boil an egg from the falcon's nest, then replace it in the nest, and secrete oneself near by with a cross-bow, under a red and white umbrella, until the mother bird, finding one of her eggs resists all her endeavors to infuse warmth into it, flies off, and plunges into the nearest fire, and returns with this ring in her beak. With Schamir she will touch

the boiled egg, and so restore the egg to its former
condition.   At that moment she must be shot, and
the ring be secured, before the falcon returns the
talisman to its owner, who is"—here Alianora made
an incomprehensible sign—"who is Queen Freydis
of Audela."

"Come," said Manuel, "what is the good of my
knowing this in the dead of winter! It will be
months before the falcons are nesting again."

"Manuel, Manuel, there is no understanding you!
Do you not see how badly it looks for a grown man,
and far more for a famed champion and a potent
sorcerer, to be pouting and scowling and kicking
your heels about like that, and having no patience
at all?"

"Yes, I suppose it does look badly, but I am
Manuel, and I follow—"

"Oh, spare me that," cried Alianora, "or else, no
matter how much I may love you, dearest, I shall
box your jaws!"

"None the less, what I was going to say is true,"
declared Manuel, "and if only you would believe it,
matters would go more smoothly between us."

II.

Magic of the Apsarasas

NOW the tale tells how, to humor Alianora, Count Manuel applied himself to the magic of the Apsarasas. He went with the Princess to a high secret place, and Alianora, crying sweetly, in the famous old fashion, "Torolix, Ciccabau, Tio, Tio, Torolililix!" performed the proper incantations, and forthwith birds came multitudinously from all quarters of the sky, in a descending flood of color and flapping and whistling and screeching.

And the peacock screamed, "With what measure thou judgest others, thou shalt thyself be judged."

Sang the nightingale, "Contentment is the greatest happiness."

The turtle-dove called, "It were better for some created things that they had never been created."

The peewit chirped, "He that hath no mercy for others, shall find none for himself."

The stork said huskily, "The fashion of this world passeth away."

And the wail of the eagle was, "However long life may be, yet its inevitable term is death."

"Now that is virtually what I said," declared the stork, "and you are a bold-faced and bald-headed plagiarist."

"And you," replied the eagle, clutching the stork's throat, "are a dead bird that will deliver no more babies."

But Dom Manuel tugged at the eagle's wing, and asked him if he really meant that to hold good before this Court of the Birds. And when the infuriated eagle opened his cruel beak, and held up one murderous claw, to make solemn oath that indeed he did mean it, and would show them too, the stork very intelligently flew away.

"I shall not ever forget your kindness, Count Manuel," cried the stork, "and do you remember that the customary three wishes are always yours for the asking."

"And I too am grateful," said the abashed eagle, —"yes, upon the whole, I am grateful, for if I had killed that long-legged pest it would have been in contempt of the court, and they would have set me to hatching red cockatrices. Still, his reproach was not unfounded, and I must think up a new cry."

So the eagle perched on a rock, and said tentatively, "There is such a thing as being too proud to fight." He shook his bald head disgustedly, and tried, "The only enduring peace is a peace without

victory," but that did not seem to content him either.
Afterward he cried out, "All persons who oppose
me have pigmy minds," and "If everybody does
not do exactly as I order, the heart of the world
will be broken": and many other foolish things he
repeated, and shook his head over, for none of these
axioms pleased the eagle.

So in his worried quest for a saying sufficiently
orotund and meaningless to be hailed with con-
venience as a great moral principle, the eagle forgot
all about Count Manuel: but the stork did not forget, because in the eyes of the stork the life of the
stork is valuable.

The other birds uttered various such sentiments
as have been recorded, and all these, they told Manuel, were accredited sorceries. The big yellow-
haired boy did not dispute it, he rarely disputed anything: but the droop to that curious left eye of his
was accentuated, and he admitted to Alianora that
he wondered if such faint-hearted smug little truths
were indeed the height of wisdom, outside of religion and public speaking. Then he asked which
was the wisest of the birds, and they told him the
Zhar-Ptitza, whom others called the Fire-Bird.

Manuel induced Alianora to summon the Zhar-
Ptitza, who is the oldest and the most learned of
all living creatures, although he has thus far learned
nothing assuredly except that appearances have to

be kept up. The Zhar-Ptitza came, crying wearily, "Fine feathers make fine birds." You heard him from afar.

The Zhar-Ptitza himself had every reason to get comfort out of this axiom, for his plumage was everywhere the most brilliant purple, except that his neck feathers were the color of new gold, and his tail was blue with somewhat longer red feathers intermingled. His throat was wattled gorgeously, and his head was tufted, and he seemed a trifle larger than the eagle. The Fire-Bird brought with him his nest of cassia and sprigs of incense, and this he put down upon the lichened rocks, and he sat in it while he talked with Manuel.

The frivolous question that Manuel raised as to his clay figures, the Zhar-Ptitza considered a very human bit of nonsense: and the wise creature said he felt forced to point out that no intelligent bird would ever dream of making images.

"But, sir," said Manuel, "I do not wish to burden this world with any more lifeless images. Instead, I wish to make in this world an animated figure, very much as, they say, a god did once upon a time—"

"Come, you should not try to put too much responsibility upon Jahveh," protested the Zhar-Ptitza, tolerantly, "for Jahveh made only one man, and did not ever do it again. I remember the making of that first man very clearly, for I was created the morning before with instructions to fly above the earth in the open firmament of heaven, so I saw the whole affair. Yes, Jahveh did create the first man on the sixth day. And I voiced no criticism. For of course after working continuously for nearly a whole week, and making so many really important things, no creative artist should be blamed for not being in his happiest vein on the sixth day."

"And did you happen to notice, sir," asks Manuel, hopefully, "by what method animation was given to Adam?"

"No, he was drying out in the sun when I first saw him, with Gabriel sitting at his feet, playing on a flageolet: and naturally I did not pay any particular attention to such foolishness."

"Well, well, I do not assert that the making of men is the highest form of art, but, none the less, a geas is upon me to make myself a very splendid and admirable young man."

"But why should you be wasting your small portion of breath and strength? To what permanent use could one put a human being even if the creature were virtuous and handsome to look at? Ah, Manuel, you have not seen them pass, as I have seen them pass in swarms, with their wars and their reforms and their great causes, and leaving nothing but their bones behind them."

"Yes, yes, to you, at your age, who were old when Nineveh was planned, it must seem strange; and I do not know why my mother desired that I should make myself a splendid and admirable young man. But the geas is upon me."

The Zhar-Ptitza sighed. "Certainly these feminine whims are not easily explained. But your people have some way of making brand-new men and women of all sorts. I am sure of this, for otherwise the race would have been extinct a great while since at the rate they kill each other. And perhaps they do adhere to Jahveh's method, and make fresh human beings out of earth, for, now I think of it, I have seen the small, recently completed ones, who looked exactly like red clay."

"It is undeniable that babies do have something of that look," assented Manuel. "So then, at least, you think I may be working in the proper medium?"

"It seems plausible, because I am certain your people are not intelligent enough to lay eggs, nor could, of course, such an impatient race succeed in getting eggs hatched. At all events, they have undoubtedly contrived some method or other, and you might find out from the least foolish of them about that method."

"Who, then, is the least foolish of mankind?"

"Probably King Helmas of Albania, for it was prophesied by me a great while ago that he would